AMAZING ALLSTAR
HOCKEY ACTIVITY BOOK

for
RUTH PORTER

Jesse, Noah and Julian Ross

Polestar Book Publishers acknowledges the ongoing support of The Canada Council, the British Columbia Ministry of Small Business, Tourism and Culture, and the Department of Canadian Heritage.

Illustrations by Anne Degrace
Cover design by Jim Brennan
Cover photographs by Chris Relke
Printed and bound in Canada

Canadian Cataloguing in Publication Data
Ross, Jesse, 1986-
The amazing allstar hockey activity book
ISBN 1-896095-92-5
1. Hockey — Juvenile literature. I. Ross, Julian, 1952- II. Ross, Noah, 1982- III. Title.
GV847.25.R668 1998 j796.962 C98-910620-9

POLESTAR BOOK PUBLISHERS
P.O. Box 5238, Station B
Victoria, British Columbia
Canada V8R 6N4
http://mypage.direct.ca/p/polestar/

In the United States:
POLESTAR BOOK PUBLISHERS
P.O. Box 468
Custer, WA
USA 98240-0468

5 4 3 2 1

Amazing Allstar Hockey Activity Book

QUIZZES

FEATURES

PUZZLES

RADICAL STATS

17
3
22

LOGO LINGO

Most NHL logos are pretty straightforward. The Toronto Maple Leafs have a maple leaf on their logo; the Mighty Ducks of Anaheim have one mean duck. You get the picture. But some of the teams have interesting items on their logos you might have missed.

Match these logo items with the city name:

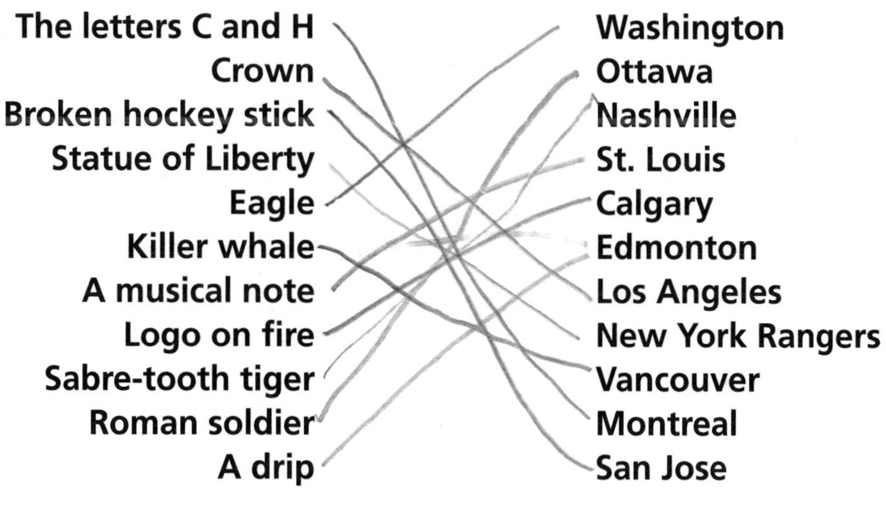

This is the logo for the NHL expansion team that starts playing in the 1999-2000 season. What is their name?

ATLANTA THRASHERS

TOP GUNS

We've hidden the last names of the highest scorers (minimum 70 points) in the 1997-98 regular season. Some teams have more than one high scorer, some have none. The names of the high scorers are written either forwards or backwards, and placed horizontally, vertically or diagonally.

The remaining 35 letters, taken from the top and going left to right, spell out the last names of five key players on the 1996-97 and 1997-98 Stanley Cup-winning Detroit Red Wings.

Jason ALLISON
Tony AMONTE
Rod BRIND'AMOUR
Peter BONDRA
Pavel BURE
Theoren FLEURY
Peter FORSBERG

Ron FRANCIS
Wayne GRETZKY
Brett HULL
Jaromir JAGR
John LECLAIR
Eric LINDROS
Adam OATES

Zigmund PALFFY
Mark RECCHI
Teemu SELANNE
Jozef STUMPEL
Mats SUNDIN
Doug WEIGHT
Alexi YASHIN

List the five Detroit Red Wings:

THE ORIGINAL ROCKET

Before Pavel Bure became known as the Russian Rocket, there was only one Rocket in NHL history — Maurice "Rocket" Richard. Beginning in the 1998-99 season, a new trophy in Rocket Richard's name will be given out to the league's leading goal-scorer. Who knows? Maybe the Russian Rocket will be the first winner!

During the 1940s and 1950s, Maurice Richard was the most famous player on the most famous team in hockey, the Montreal Canadiens. He is also the only player in hockey history to be the cause of a full-scale riot. It happened on March 17, 1955 during a game at the Montreal Forum. The Rocket wasn't there that night because he had received a suspension for the remainder of the season and playoffs for punching a linesman during a fight in a previous game. But the league commissioner was in attendance, and the Rocket's fans were outraged at their hero's fate. They pelted the commissioner with debris, set off a tear-gas bomb and charged into the streets of Montreal, rioting and looting until 3 a.m.

Maurice Richard led the Canadiens to eight Stanley Cups and in the 1944-45 season became the first player ever to score 50 goals in 50 games. A pure goal-scorer, he never led the league in points, though he often led the league in goals. And once, during a 5-1 playoff victory over Toronto in which he scored all five goals, the three-star selection was Richard, Richard and Richard!

TUROFSKY—IMPERIAL OIL / HOCKEY HALL OF FAME

Former goalie Don Simmons said of the Rocket, "There was just no stopping him. When he was bearing down on you, his eyes shone like headlights on a truck. It was terrifying."

COMMON GROUND

Even though there are now many professional hockey leagues at different levels playing in North America, Europe and Asia, the hockey world is still pretty small.

What do the following hockey people have in common?

1 Jari Kurri, Sari Fisk and Teemu Selanne:

- ☐ All three won the Calder Rookie-of-the-Year Trophy.
- ☒ They all played hockey for Finland in the 1998 Winter Olympics.
- ☐ They all played on the same team in juniors.
- ☐ They've all appeared in those "Milk" ads.

2 Jacques Lemaire, Larry Robinson and Marc Crawford:

- ☐ They all went to the same elementary school.
- ☐ They are all recent Boston draft picks.
- ☐ They all list their favourite sport as bowling.
- ☒ All of them have been both NHL players and coaches.

3 Martin Brodeur, Rick Knickle and Patrick Lalime:

- ☐ They've all refereed at least one NHL game.
- ☐ They are cousins.
- ☒ They've all played goal in the NHL.
- ☐ They've all scored a goal in the NHL.

4 Wayne Gretzky, Kelly Hrudey and Chris Marinucci:

- [x] They have all played on the Los Angeles Kings.
- [ ] None of them played a hockey game until they were 21.
- [ ] They all have restaurants named after them.
- [ ] They all said they would retire after the 1997-98 season.

5 Manon Rheaume, Vicky Sunohara and Sarah Teuting:

- [ ] They have all had an NHL tryout.
- [x] They all won medals in the 1998 Winter Olympics in Nagano.
- [ ] All are goalies.
- [ ] All have pet crocodiles.

6 Ted Nolan, Pat Burns, Brian Sutter and Scotty Bowman:

- [ ] They all played together on the 1976-77 Cleveland Barons.
- [ ] They have all coached the Buffalo Sabres.
- [x] They have all won the Jack Adams Trophy for coach of the year.
- [ ] They have all won the Stanley Cup as a coach.

7 John Davidson, Greg Millen and John Garrett:

- [ ] As NHL goalies, they've all lost more games than they've won.
- [ ] They are all *Hockey Night in Canada* commentators.
- [ ] They were all goalies in the NHL.
- [x] All of the above.

8 Brian Bellows, Jeremy Roenick, Tony Amonte and Cliff Ronning:

- [x] They have all played professional hockey in Europe.
- [ ] They all played for Team Canada in the 1998 Winter Olympics.
- [ ] They were all former junior stars of the Guelph Storm team in the Ontario Hockey League.
- [ ] They all list tofu dogs as their favourite food.

THE FACES OF HOCKEY

It's an important face-off, late in the third period, deep in the opponent's zone. The camera zooms in. The player gazes straight ahead, focussing intently on the job at hand. Mark Messier. Doug Gilmour. Tie Domi. The faces of hockey are becoming the icons of the game.

Match the following faces with the names of the players listed below.

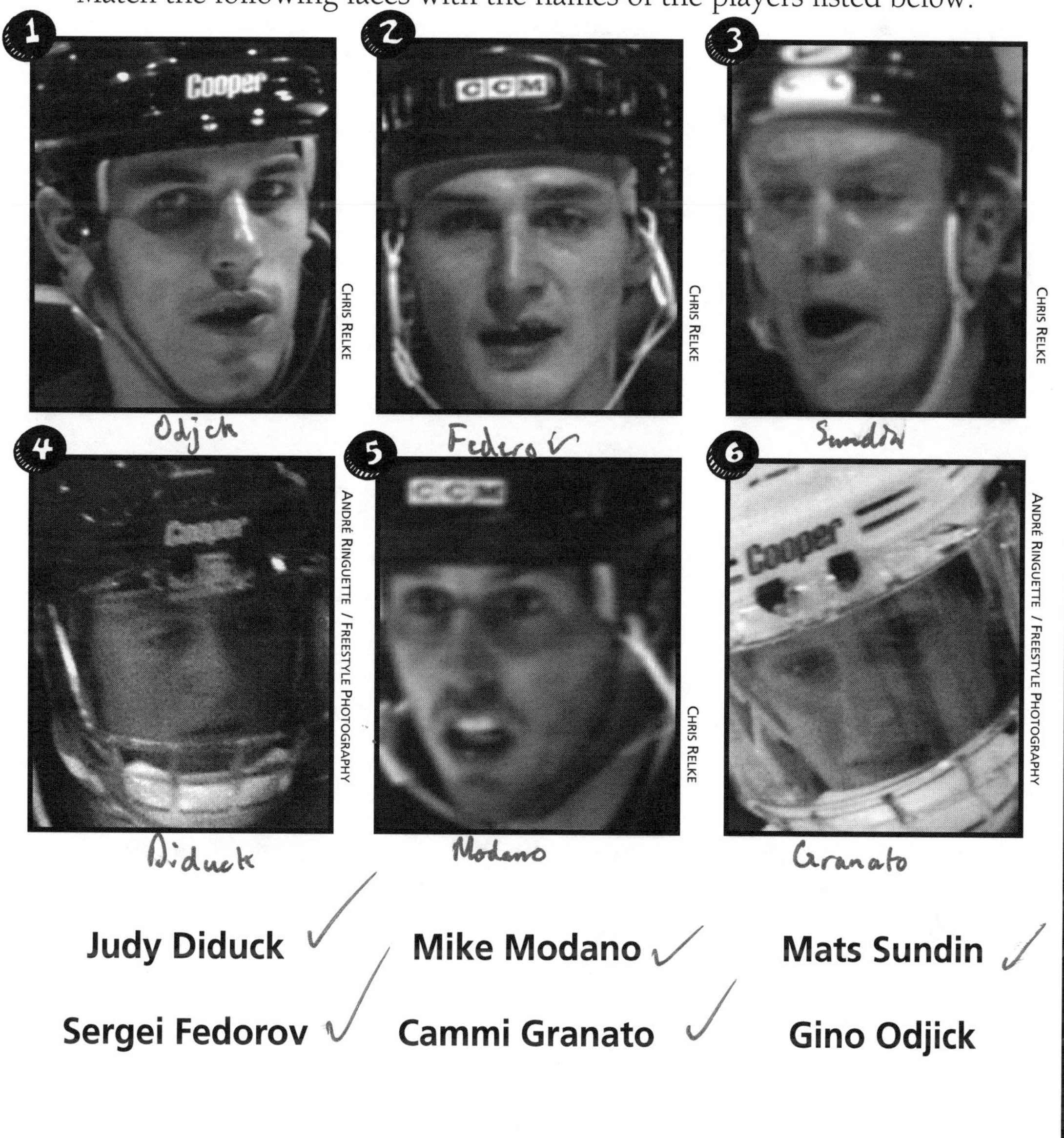

CHRIS RELKE / CHRIS RELKE / CHRIS RELKE / ANDRÉ RINGUETTE / FREESTYLE PHOTOGRAPHY / CHRIS RELKE / ANDRÉ RINGUETTE / FREESTYLE PHOTOGRAPHY

Judy Diduck **Mike Modano** **Mats Sundin**

Sergei Fedorov **Cammi Granato** **Gino Odjick**

HOCKEY WEBSITES

Hey Net Surfers! We've compiled tons of hockey websites, ranging from fan pages to The Hockey Hall of Fame to great women's hockey sites to Official Team Pages — and lots more. Our crew has made notes on each page and we've rated each site as follows:

An outstanding work-of-art;
A very good page, definitely worth checking out;
An above-average page with some ups and downs;
Might be of some interest to the occasional surfer;
A poorly done page, with barely anything interesting on the whole site.

We've categorized the pages into two sections: "Official" and "Other/News/ Fan." But remember, websites change. A poorly done page could get a makeover ... and become an excellent site. **Please note: all addresses start with http://**

Official Websites:

Anaheim Mighty Ducks www.mightyducks.com 
Not much stuff, only 4 sections. Check out "Fan Forum."

Atlanta Thrashers www.atlantathrashers.com
Good setup, OK updates, good page considering they won't be in the NHL until 1999-2000.

Boston Bruins www.bostonbruins.com
Great updates, fast, well-organized. Check out "Meet the Bruins" — it has excellent info on players, coaches, prospects and other neat stuff.

Buffalo Sabres www.sabres.com
Good setup, easy to get at. "Links" is a nice section. Above average, but something lacking.

Calgary Flames **www.calgaryflames.com** 
Easy to access what you want, but a bit boring.

Canadian Womens Hockey
www.canadianhockey.ca/ntwom.html 
Rosters, championship details. Official, but dull.

Carolina Hurricanes **www.carolinahurricanes.com** 
Great updates, but not enough stuff overall.
Check out "Face-Off" for bulletin boards and feedback.

Chicago Blackhawks **www.chicagoblackhawks.com** 
Good multimedia section, but otherwise a bad page.

Colorado Avalanche **www.coloradoavalanche.com**
Slow, without good updates. "Players" section is badly done.

Dallas Stars **www.dallasstars.com** 
Slow, frames, lots of ads; kind of hard to find what you want. Check out "The Fan" for multimedia, bulletin boards, trivia.

Detroit Red Wings **www.detroitredwings.com** 
Good news section, easy to get what you want, lots of info.
Check out "Game Day" for chat, archives, photos etc.

Edmonton Oilers **www.edmontonoilers.com** 
Slow, plus an ad that takes up one-third of the page.
Check out "Fan Forum" for trivia and some other fun stuff.

Florida Panthers **www.flpanthers.com** 
Lots of info on players and well-designed.

LA Kings **www.lakings.com/Kings/ind.html** 

Great updates, quick and comprehensive, but not much stuff. Check out “Fan Forum” — it’s good.

Montreal Canadiens **www.canadiens.com/english/** 

Good updates, very slow, okay page, not much fun. Check out “Multimedia” for an email club, some movies etc.

Nashville Predators **www.nash-nhl.com** 

Excellent news section and frames. “Trivia” is very hard but there are cool prizes. Check out “Fun Stuff” — it’s fun stuff!

New Jersey Devils **www.newjerseydevils.com** 

Shockwave Flash is necessary to view this page — don’t come here without it.

New York Islanders **www.xice.com** 

Very comprehensive stats package, but not very well designed.

New York Rangers **www.newyorkrangers.com** 

Pretty good page, but nothing special. Check out “Kids Club”; for $15 you get a bunch of cool stuff.

NHL **www.nhl.com** 

Official home-page of the NHL: scores, stats, schedule, news etc. Not a very cool page.

Ottawa Senators **www.ottawasenators.com**  

Fast, well-organized and “The Quiz” is hard (but fun). Check out “Fans of all Ages” — it has a scrapbook, contests, hockey hodge-podge and some things to download. It’s a lot of fun.

Philadelphia Flyers **www.philadelphiaflyers.com**
Page was under construction when we checked.

Phoenix Coyotes **www.nhlcoyotes.com** 
Nice layout, but not much pizzazz. Check out "Game Day" and "On the Air."

Pittsburgh Penguins **www.pittsburghpenguins.com** 
Okay page but no trivia or fan section and there are lots of ads. Check out "Another Chapter in Sports" for books on the Pens.

San Jose Sharks **www.sj-sharks.com/**  
Quick, great updates, good info, nice news area. Check out the "1-on-1" section — it has a bunch of cool stuff.

St. Louis Blues **www.stlouisblues.com/home.html** 
Very slow page, but has good updates and a cool "Just for Kids" section.

Tampa Bay Lightning **www.tampabaylightning.com** 
Slow, good updates, decent page — but still a bit boring.

Toronto Maple Leafs **www.torontomapleleafs.com** 
Nice background, good updates, lots about the Gardens, good news section. Check out "Bud's Club," a cool club for kids.

Vancouver Canucks **www.orcabay.com/canucks/index.html**
Great-looking page, but slow and not enough info.

Washington Capitals **www.washingtoncaps.com** 
Good updates and quick loading time, but has nothing special and is kind of boring. But check out "Records" — it's very good.

Other/News/Fan Websites:

Andria Hunter's Women's Hockey Page ●●●●●

www.cs.utoronto.ca/~andria/womens_hockey-info.html

Done by Andria Hunter, a former Gold Medalist on the Canadian Women's National Team. Has *amazing* links to everything you could ever want to know about women's hockey.

CBS Sportsline **www.sportsline.com/nhl/index.html** ●●●●

Updated daily, fast, a great source for news, scores, stats etc. Good page but nothing new.

Drop The Gloves **ernie.bgsu.edu/~rchadwi/fighters/pugilist** 
Bad updates, but lots of pictures and movies. If you don't like fighting or fighters, don't come here.

ESPNET **espnnet.sportszone.com/nhl/** 
Very frequent updates, organized, the best source for news, scores, summaries, stats etc. Check out "The Wire" for up to the minute news and articles.

NHL 4 Kids.com **www.nhl4kids.com** 
Frames, lot's of fun stuff for kids. Worth a look.

Painted Warrior
users.aol.com/maskman30/pwhpnf.html 
A fantastic site for goalie buffs! Includes history of goaltending and a huge photo gallery of classic, minor and pro hockey masks.

Professional Hockey Server
maxwell.uhh.hawaii.edu/hockey/teams.html 
Want a quick link to your favourite team? Check this out!

SLAM sports: Women's Hockey
www.canoe.com/HockeyWomen/home.html 
Fast, up-to-date, lots of news/headlines etc. Great source for women's hockey news and info.

The Hockey News **www.thn.com** 
Great updates, lots of stuff on their newspaper, but not much fun.

TSN **www.tsn.ca/nhl/** 
Frames, excellent news, the usual stats, scores. Check out "Hockey Chat."

WHO AM I?

Hailed by some as the best female hockey player in the world, this Saskatchewan centre was invited by the Philadelphia Flyers to their summer prospects camp in July 1998. She has played on the Canadian Women's National Team since she was 16, helping them win gold medals at the last two World Championships, plus an Olympic silver medal in Nagano, Japan.

PHILLIP MACCALLUM / FREESTYLE PHOTOGRAPHY

_ _ _ _ _ _ _ _ _ _ _ _ _ _ _ _ _ _ _ _

GONE BUT NOT FORGOTTEN

The NHL started in 1917-18, more than 80 years ago. Since then there have been 44 different teams in 34 different cities. In some of those cities, like Cleveland and Hamilton, teams played for just a short period of time and NHL hockey has never returned. But other cities, like Ottawa and Pittsburgh, got a second chance when, some 60 years later, their teams came back.

Your task is to try to match the names of these defunct teams with the cities they played in. One hint: the Whalers did *not* play in Colorado.

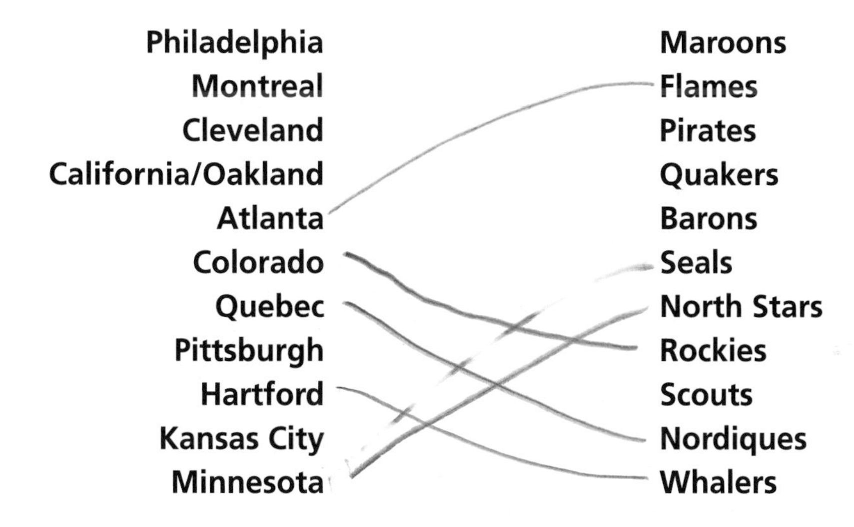

This is the logo of an NHL team that played in an American city in the mid-1970s. NHL hockey will return to that city in 1999-2000. Which team's logo was this?

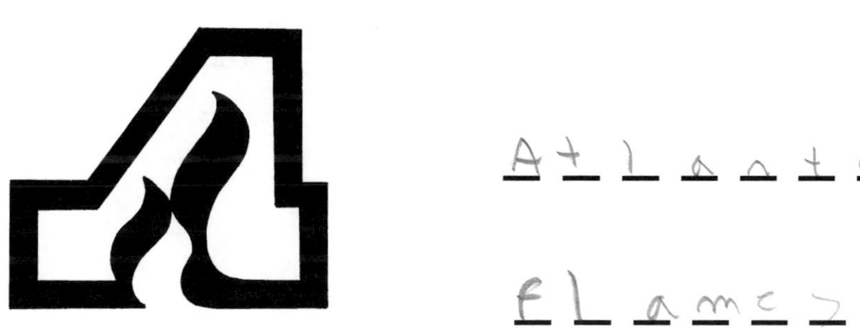

HOCKEY STARS

We've hidden the last names of many of the world's top female hockey stars. Their names are written either forwards or backwards, and placed horizontally, vertically or diagonally. The remaining 19 letters, taken from the top and going left to right, spell out the nickname of Guo Hong, the amazing goalie for the Chinese women's team.

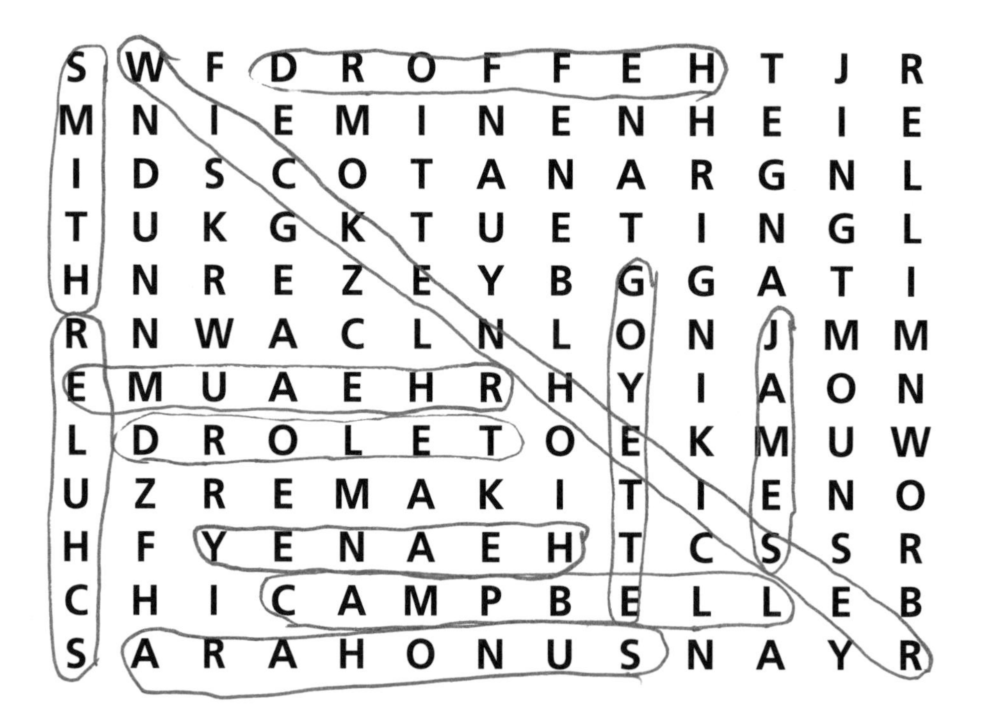

CANADIAN

Cassie CAMPBELL
Nancy DROLET
Danielle GOYETTE
Geraldine HEANEY
Jayna HEFFORD
Angela JAMES
Manon RHEAUME
Laura SCHULER
Fiona SMITH
Vicky SUNOHARA
Hayley WICKENHEISER

AMERICAN

Lisa BROWNMILLER
Karyn BYE
Tricia DUNN
Cammi GRANATO
Katie KING
Sue MERZ
A.J. MLECZKO
Tara MOUNSEY
Sarah TUETING

FINNISH

Sari FISK
Riika NIEMINEN

CHINESE

Zhang JING

JAPANESE

Tsuchida AKI

Nickname of GUO HONG:

_ _ _   _ _ _ _ _ _   _ _ _ _

_ _   _ _ _ _ _

Vicki Movsessian of Team USA fends off Team Canada's Hayley Wickenheiser.

PHILLIP MACCALLUM / FREESTYLE PHOTOGRAPHY

BRINGING HOME THE HARDWARE

Teams. Players. Coaches. They all are eligible for awards, often on a weekly or monthly basis. Some awards, like the Hart Memorial Trophy for most valuable player, have been around since the early 1920s and are steeped in hockey tradition; others, like the Mastercard Cutting Edge Player of the Year Trophy or the Bud Ice Plus-Minus Award have been created only recently, mostly at the urging of advertisers.

With the recent announcement of the new Rocket Richard Award, some people want to change the award names to honour players — for example, change the best defenceman award to the Bobby Orr Trophy, or create new awards to honour Gordie Howe or Wayne Gretzky.

Let's see if you're ready to skate a victory lap holding the Stanley Cup over your head. Test yourself with this quiz about awards.

1. Only one player pictured on the front cover of this book has won the Calder Trophy for Rookie of the Year. Which one?
   - ❑ Dominik Hasek
   - ❑ Cammi Granato
   - ☑ Pavel Bure
   - ❑ Joe Sakic

2. If a player wins a major trophy like the Hart, Vezina, Calder or the Conn Smythe, what else do they receive?
   - ☑ $1,000
   - ❑ induction into the Hockey Hall of Fame
   - ❑ a trip to Disneyland
   - ❑ $10,000

3. The trophy awarded to the top team at the Canadian National Women's Championship is named in honour of:
   - ❑ Hobey Baker
   - ❑ Rose Cherry
   - ☒ Abby Hoffman
   - ❑ Angela James

4. The trophy for coach of the year is named after:
   - ❑ Jack Daniels
   - ☑ Jack Adams
   - ❑ Scotty Bowman
   - ❑ Don Cherry

5. The Jennings Trophy is awarded to:
   - ❑ the best defensive pairing in the league
   - ❑ the most popular referee, as chosen by the players
   - ❑ the player with the most assists
   - ☒ the goalie or goalies playing on the team with the fewest goals against (having played in a minimum of 25 games)

6. At the end of his rookie season, Wayne Gretzky was tied with Marcel Dionne for the scoring lead, but Gretzky didn't win the Art Ross trophy, Dionne did. Why?
   - ❑ Dionne scored more goals
   - ❑ they flipped a coin, and Gretzky lost
   - ❑ D came before G in the alphabet
   - ☑ Dionne was older than Gretzky

7. The Presidents' Trophy is awarded to:
   - ❑ the best American team in the NHL
   - ☒ the team with the best regular-season record
   - ❑ the top American-born player
   - ❑ the fastest skater at the NHL Skills Competition

PUZZLING PICTURES

These drawings represent the names of current NHL players, plus the nickname of one player. If a letter in the answer is already filled in, the illustration refers to the last name only.

1 

JOE THORNTON

2 

STEVE YZERMAN

3 

RUSSIAN ROCKET

4 

DOUG WEIGHT

5 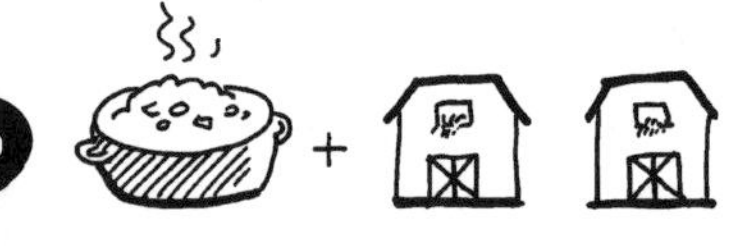

STU BARNES

6 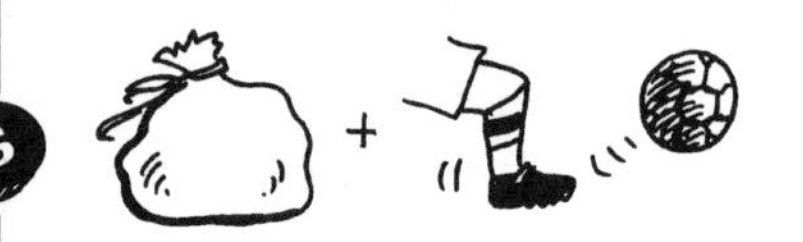

JOE SAKIC

7 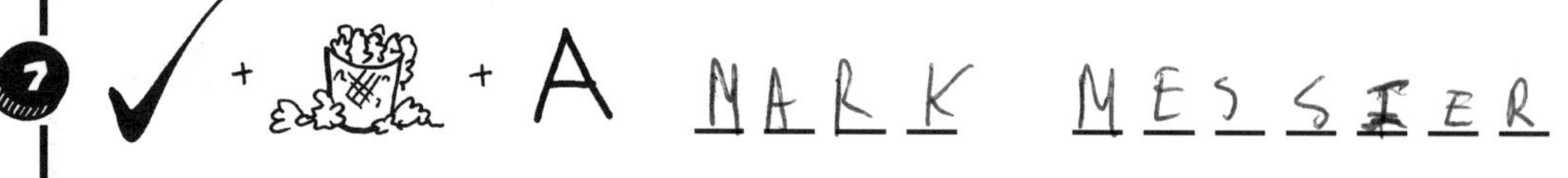

IT'S A NUMBERS GAME

Match the records on the left with their correct numbers on the right. (Note: these records were accurate to the end of the 1997-98 regular season.)

Record for most goals in a career (Wayne Gretzky)	**15**
Longest undefeated streak by a team (Philadelphia Flyers)	**1**
Most penalty minutes in a career (Tiger Williams)	**1,818**
Fewest home losses in a modern-day season (70+ games) (Montreal Canadiens)	**885**
Number of players drafted in the 1998 Entry Draft	**35**
Most points in one period (Bryan Trottier)	**103**
Most games played in a career (Gordie Howe)	**3,966**
Number of registered women hockey players in North America	**1,767**
Most Hart Trophies won by one player (Wayne Gretzky)	**10**
Most shutouts in a career (Terry Sawchuk)	**53,317**
Most 20+ goal-scorers on one team in a year (Boston Bruins)	**11**
Most games coached by one coach (Scotty Bowman)	**258**
Number of seconds it took to score the fastest goal in a rookie's first NHL game (Gus Bodnar)	**6**

HOCKEY HEADLINES

Headline writers love puns, and the cornier the better:

Lightning Strikes Again!

Rangers See Stars!

Hurricane Carolina Destroys Edmonton!

Flames Burn Leafs!

If you're a Colorado fan, you'd be all too familiar with "**Avalanche Buries Boston**" or Ottawa or Vancouver.

With three new expansion teams — the Minnesota Wild, Atlanta Thrashers and Columbus Bluejackets — about to enter the NHL, sportswriters around the league are gearing up for a brand new batch of silly headlines. Using these new team names, see if you can come up with some fun headlines of your own.

Sharks Bite Penguins!

RADICAL STATS

I Get Knocked Down But I Get Up Again

Life as a fighter in the NHL is no walk in the park. There's always some cocky young brawler who wants to take your place and you rarely get a chance to prove that you are more than just a tough guy. After every fight your knuckles are swollen and sore, but if you stop fighting you're history. Once you're seen as a fourth-liner who gets between two and four minutes of ice time per period, it's hard to "break the mould" and prove that you also have the offensive skills to help your team win the game. There are some fighters who have become capable checkers and even goal-scorers — Randy McKay, Dale Hunter, Brad May and Joe Kocur, to name a few — but most fighters spend their career being typecast. They are rarely, if ever, given the chance to become anything more.

The chart on the next page compares the 10 players who had the most fights in the 1997-98 regular season. For instance, Donald Brashear, who led the league in penalty minutes with 372, had the most points of any of the fighters on this list. Krzysztof Oliwa, a Polish-born 6' 5" 235-pound left winger who played in the American, International and East Coast minor pro leagues before finally joining the NHL with the New Jersey Devils, had significantly fewer penalty minutes than Brashear, but more fighting majors. Oliwa led the league with 32 fights, averaging a fight every 2.28 games.

CHRIS RELKE

Donald Brashear, the 6' 2" 220-pound left winger of the Vancouver Canucks.

RADICAL STATS

Team	Player	GP	FM	PIM	G/P	AGBF
NJD	K. Oliwa	73	32	295	2/5	2.28
CA	J. Odgers	68	26	213	5/13	2.62
VC	D. Brashear	77	26	372	9/18	2.96
TML	T. Domi	80	24	365	4/14	3.33
FP	P. Laus	77	23	293	0/11	3.35
LAK	M. Johnson	66	21	249	2/6	3.14
CH	S. Grimson	82	20	204	3/7	4.1
TML	K. King	82	19	199	3/6	4.32
BB	K. Baumgartner	82	19	199	0/1	4.32
PF	D. Kordic	61	18	210	1/2	3.38

GP = games played • FM = number of fighting majors • PIM = penalties in minutes • G/P = goals/points • AGBF = average games between fights

Unusual Stats — Did you know:

- During both the 1996-97 and 1997-98 seasons, the Ottawa Senators were the least penalized team. In both years they accumulated identical penalty totals — 1107 minutes.

- In the 1997-98 season, left wingers Ken Baumgartner of the Bruins and Kris King of the Leafs both had 19 fights, 199 penalty minutes and played 82 games. Incidentally, they both were born in Canada in 1966, entered the NHL in the 1987-88 season and shoot left.

- During the 1997-98 regular season, in games where Dallas winger Jere Lehtinen scored a goal his team never lost.

Name that Player!

Obviously, it doesn't matter what your name is — it's how you play the game that counts! Still we thought it would be interesting to see if the top point-getters shared a first name as well as great skills. We went through the top 250 scorers in the 1997-98 regular season and here's a list of how many of those players share the most popular names. See how many of these players you know already — players like Steve Yzerman, Brian Leetch, Sergei Federov. If you don't find *your* name on this list, don't worry — Pavel, Jaromir, Wayne, Brett and Theoren aren't on the list either.

- Steve 8
- Brian, Bryan 8
- Geoff, Jeff 7
- Robert, Rob 7
- Alexi 5
- Scott 5
- Mike 5
- Sergei 4
- Joe 4
- Martin 4
- Eric 4
- Jason 4
- Dave 4
- Kevin 3
- Tony 3
- Doug 3
- Chris 3
- Alexander, Alex 3
- Bill 3
- Paul 3
- Adam 3
- Ray 3
- Gary 3

CHRIS RELKE

Steve Yzerman (left), captain of the Detroit Red Wings, with teammate Brendan Shanahan. Yzerman was the Conn Smythe Trophy winner as the 1998 playoff MVP.

RADICAL STATS

The Tall and the Short of It

It's no secret — NHL players are getting bigger. Power forwards like Philadelphia's 220-pounders John LeClair (6'2") and Eric Lindros (6'4"), Keith Tkachuk of the Coyotes and Detroit's Brendan Shanahan have revolutionized the game. They've combined banging and crashing with a goal-scorer's touch.

Teams now place great importance on developing a bigger defence corps. Veteran defensive giants Uwe Krupp and Kjell Samuelsson, both 6'6" and 235 pounds, have recently been joined by two even taller rookie defensemen — the Islanders' Zdeno Chara (6'8") and Vancouver's Chris McCallister (6'7").

Fortunately, speed and skill are still valued. Explosive wingers like Sergei Samsonov (5'8"), Boston's Calder Trophy winner, or Theoren Fleury (5'6"), Calgary's feisty allstar, plus small playmaking centres like Cliff Ronning and Ray Whitney help a team create the desired combination of speed and strength.

Goaltenders make up the largest percentage of smaller-sized players in the NHL. While there *are* some tall goalies, many netminders are much shorter than six feet. John Vanbiesbrouck, Chris Terreri and Arturs Irbe are only 5'8".

Imagine a penalty-shot showdown between 5'8" 165-pound award-winning goalie Mike Vernon and Peter Worrell, a 6'6" 250-pound Florida Panthers bruiser ... Despite the size difference, we'd still give Vernon the advantage!

RADICAL STATS

Scoring Down, Way Down

Since Wayne Gretzky's all-time high of 215 points in the 1985-86 season, scoring has fallen dramatically. In 1997-98, Jaromir Jagr lead the league with 102 points — and Jagr was the only player to break the 100-point mark.

To illustrate this downward trend, we've put together the number of 70, 80, 90 and 100-point scorers from the 1997-98 season, the 1996-97 season, the 1992-93 season and the 1985-86 season (the year that Gretzky scored 215 points, more than double Jaromir Jagr's output for the 1997-98 season).

1985-86 season

13 100-point scorers
19 90-point scorers
31 80-point scorers
62 70-point scorers

1992-93 season

9 100-point scorers
17 90-point scorers
29 80-point scorers
53 70-point scorers

1996-97 season

2 100-point scorers
9 90-point scorers
21 80-point scorers
32 70-point scorers

1997-98 season

1 100-point scorer
4 90-point scorers
9 80-point scorers
21 70-point scorers

You probably noticed that the biggest difference in scoring is between the 1985-86 season and the 1997-98 season. Last year there was only one 100-point scorer and there were only 21 70-point scorers. Twelve years previously, in 1985-86, there were 13 100-point scorers and 62 70-point scorers. This means there were almost three times as many 70-point scorers in 1986. This is even more amazing when you realize that in 1985-86 there were fewer teams (21 compared to 26 in 1997-98) and almost 100 fewer players. Also, in 1985-86, teams played only 80 games — not 82 like today.

CHRIS RELKE

Jaromir Jagr, who helped the Czech Republic capture the gold medal at the 1998 Winter Olympics, led the NHL in scoring in both 1995 and 1998. He is one of the few NHLers to average more than one point per game.

If you look closer, you'll also see that although scoring was down a little bit between 1985-86 and 1992-93, the biggest dip has happened more recently, between 1992-93 and 1997-98. Even one year makes a difference. Look at 1996-97 and 1997-98 and you'll see an undeniable difference: 9 90-point scorers and 21 80-point scorers in 1996-97, and 4 90-point scorers and 9 80-point scorers in 1997-98.

Here are two good examples. In 1992-93 left winger Paul Ysebaert played 79 games for the Detroit Red Wings and got 75 points; he came third in team scoring. In 1997-98 he played 82 games for the Tampa Bay Lightning team and got far fewer points: 40 of them. This time, however, he led the team in scoring.

In 1992-93, when Jeremy Roenick was with the Chicago Blackhawks, he scored 103 points, leading his team in scoring. In 1997-98 as a member of the Phoenix Coyotes he had only 56 points but was second in team scoring.

TOTAL TRIVIA

1. Which of these Canadian cities have never had an NHL franchise?
   - ❑ Winnipeg
   - ❑ Saskatoon
   - ❑ Hamilton
   - ❑ Quebec City

2. Ed Jovanovski, the Florida defenseman who was the first choice overall in the 1994 entry draft, is nicknamed:
   - ❑ Mr. Ed
   - ❑ Jovocop
   - ❑ Cosa Noski
   - ❑ Chuckles

3. The Portland Winter Hawks won the 1998 Memorial Cup, junior hockey's highest achievement. Before the playoffs began, the team members:
   - ❑ decided not to shave during the playoffs
   - ❑ shaved their heads bald
   - ❑ dyed their hair blonde
   - ❑ tattooed the team logo on their arms

4. The NHL single-season shutout record is 22, set in 1928-29 by a Montreal Canadiens goalie. Who was he?
   - ❑ George Hainsworth
   - ❑ Ken Dryden
   - ❑ Patrick Roy
   - ❑ Tiny Thompson

5. Which of the following expansion teams had a winning record in their first season?
   - ❑ Pittsburgh Penguins
   - ❑ Florida Panthers
   - ❑ As of the 1997-98 season, no expansion team had ever had a winning record
   - ❑ Ottawa Senators

6. The record for the most points by a player in one game is 10. Who holds it?

- ❑ Wayne Gretzky
- ❑ Gordie Howe
- ❑ Jaromir Jagr
- ❑ Darryl Sittler

got it

7. Turk Broda, a very successful Toronto goalie in the 1940s and 1950s, was once threatened with being thrown off the team unless he:

- ❑ lost weight
- ❑ got a haircut
- ❑ stopped bringing his dog into the dressing room
- ❑ changed his undershirt more often

got it

8. Which current NHL goalie is nicknamed Godzilla?

- ❑ Ron Hextall
- ❑ Curtis Joseph
- ❑ Olaf Kolzig
- ❑ Em Ton

got it

3/4

FREESTYLE PHOTOGRAPHY

Before becoming one of the top NHL goalies, "Godzilla" played in the Western Hockey League, the East Coast Hockey League and the American Hockey League.

9. The record for most appearances by a coach in a Stanley Cup final is 16. Who holds it?

- ❑ Dick Irvin
- ❑ Mike Keenan
- ❑ Scotty Bowman
- ❑ Toe Blake

IT'S A FAMILY GAME

Considering the number of young hockey players who dream of making it to the NHL, the odds of a brother act succeeding are astronomical. Nonetheless, there have been some incredible brother combinations, two of which have been elected to the Hockey Hall of Fame. Maurice "Rocket" Richard played on the Canadiens with his brother, Henri, nicknamed "the Pocket Rocket." Combined, they helped Montreal win a total of 19 Stanley Cups! Tony Esposito, a goalie, played 16 seasons in the NHL in the 1970s and 80s, while his younger brother Phil, an allstar centre, was the first player to score more than 100 points in one season.

During a game in 1971, two brothers faced each other in net: Montreal's great Ken Dryden, who helped Montreal win six Cups, played against his older brother Dave, Buffalo's goalie. By far the greatest single family achievement was that of the Sutter brothers of Viking, Alberta. During the 1980s, six brothers played in the NHL: Brian, Darryl, Duane, Brent, plus twin brothers Rich and Ron.

On the hockey horizon are two young Swedes, Daniel and Henrik Sedin, identical twins expected to be chosen in the top 10 of the 1999 entry draft.

Fathers and sons have also played in the NHL. Gordie Howe, who played 26 seasons as a pro, was in both the WHA and NHL on the same team, and sometimes the same line, as his two sons Mark and Marty. Brett Hull's father Bobby was also a much-feared goal-scorer.

Now, with women's hockey becoming more prominent, there are some notable brother and sister pairs. Cammi Granato, who won an Olympic gold medal in women's hockey for the United States, has a brother, Tony, who is a longtime NHL player. Judy Diduck, a four-time gold medallist with Team Canada, plays the same position as brother Gerald, a veteran NHL defenseman.

See if you know the names of these current NHL brothers:

____________ & ____________ **Bure**

____________ & ____________ **Courtnall**

____________ & ____________ **Niedermayer**

____________ & ____________ **Mironov**

____________ & ____________ **Primeau**

Did You Know?

The highest scoring brother duo in hockey history will soon be Wayne Gretzky and his younger brother Brent, even though Brent has only scored one NHL goal to date! By the end of the 1997-98 season, Wayne had 885 goals, while Henri and Maurice Richard were holding the record at 902.

THE ART OF THE MASK

Believe it or not, goalies wearing masks is a fairly recent development in hockey history. It took a truly innovative Montreal goalie named Jacques Plante to stand up to his coaches, team management, fans and other players who thought it cowardly for a goalie to wear a mask.

On November 1, 1959, during the second period of a game against the New York Rangers, Plante stopped an Andy Bathgate shot with his face. The game was halted while Plante was stitched up (teams didn't have back-up goalies in those days) and when he returned — wearing a fiberglass mask he had built himself — the look of hockey was changed forever.

TUROFSKY—IMPERIAL OIL / HOCKEY HALL OF FAME

A 1959 photo of Jacques Plante, the Montreal Canadiens' "Masked Marvel," wearing his historic first mask.

From those humble beginnings, the art of the mask has developed dramatically. Modern goalies like Curtis Joseph (Cujo) and Olaf Kolzig (Godzilla) showcase their personalities by wearing wilder and more complex masks that use more than 20 different colours and cost upwards of $1,500.

Mask art has taken almost 40 years to get this flashy. Gerry Cheevers, a Hall of Fame goalie who helped Boston win two Stanley Cups in the early 1970s, is credited with the first mask decoration — whenever his plain white mask was hit by a puck or a stick, he'd have his trainer paint black stitches on it. Soon, most goalies started to wear masks decorated with simple one- or two-colour designs. Many of these masks were built and designed by Greg Harrison. His most famous mask, a ferocious Jungle Cat motif for Ranger goalie Gilles Gratton, is displayed at the Hockey Hall of Fame in Toronto.

These molded fiberglass masks were extremely hot to wear and, because the eye holes were open, not completely safe. Some goalies switched to helmets with a wire cage, similar to what Dominik Hasek wears today, but most goalies prefer the combination mask/cage models.

BOB MUMMERY

Grant Fuhr, who now has close to 400 NHL victories, is seen here playing for Team Canada at Rendez-Vous 1987. His mask is typical of the molded fiberglass masks worn in the 1970s and 1980s, which gave more protection to the head and face than Plante's early models.

These new combination masks also have more room for decoration. Goalies seem to love the attention a unique design brings. “It shows your individuality,” says Curtis Joseph, whose Cujo mask was patterned after a movie about a mad dog. “It says something about you.”

Working in Adobe Photoshop or similar computer programs, designers like Dennis Simone of Painted Warrior Designs in New York can create a custom design in three to four weeks at an average cost of $475 U.S. This doesn’t include the initial mask price, only the design. Chip-resistant car paint is used, plus many coats of protective lacquer.

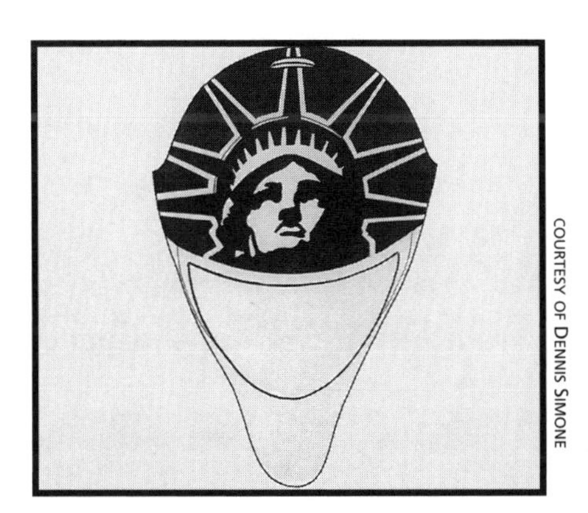

COURTESY OF DENNIS SIMONE

COURTESY OF DENNIS SIMONE

COURTESY OF DENNIS SIMONE

Before a new mask is approved, detailed computer sketches are created (left). This one, by designer Dennis Simone, is for Mike Richter of the New York Rangers. The finished mask, with a Statue of Liberty theme, is on the right.

Dennis Simone, who has designed more than 200 masks, includes Curtis Joseph, Sean Burke, Jim Carey, Mike Richter and Guy Herbert as his clients. He's also created an incredible website dedicated to the art and history of the goalie mask (the Painted Warrior website address is listed on page 19).

Simone says that many pro goalies now prefer to have an individual theme on the top of their masks and team colours on the sides and bottom. That way, if they get traded they can easily change the team colours and keep their main design intact.

Vancouver goalie Corey Hirsch's mask, a perfect example of an elaborate theme helmet, features scenes from the Alfred Hitchcock movie *Psycho*. It was designed by Dennis Simone.

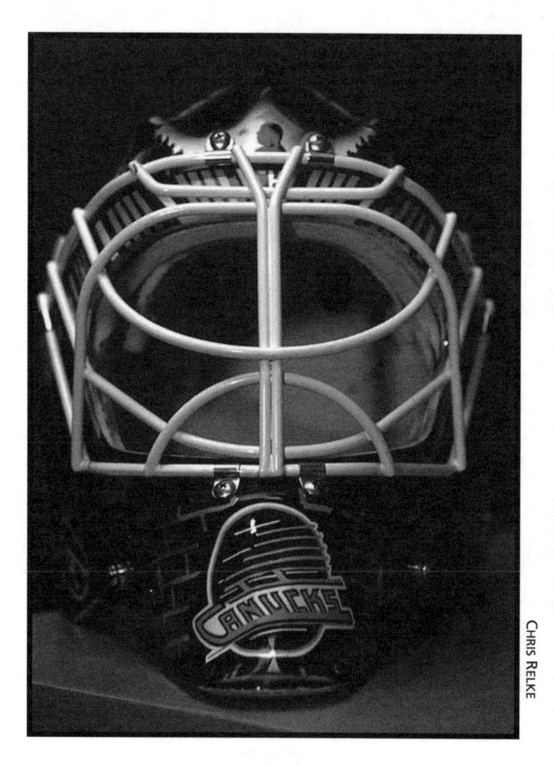

CHRIS RELKE

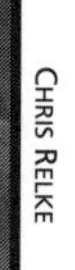

CHRIS RELKE

CHRIS RELKE

FROM SMALL-TOWN RINKS...

Craig Berube was born in Calahoo, Alberta; Bryan Berard in Woonsocket, Rhode Island; Dominik Hasek in Pardubice, Czechoslovakia. Which just proves that if you've got loads of talent, you can make it to the NHL from anywhere. In fact, NHL history shows that many stars came from small towns: Gordie Howe from Floral, Saskatchewan; Guy Lafleur from Thurso, Quebec; Lanny McDonald from Hanna, Alberta. Even today, when NHL teams are stocking up with talent from all over the world, there are still a number of big-city players who learned to play the game on small-town community rinks.

See how well you match these NHL players with their small-town roots:

Curtis Joseph	**Ornskoldsvik, Sweden**
Gino Odjick	**Carman, Manitoba, Canada**
Al MacInnis	**Espoo, Finland**
Peter Forsberg	**Kleswick, Ontario, Canada**
Geoff Sanderson	**Oxbow, Saskatchewan, Canada**
Steve Yzerman	**Cranbrook, British Columbia, Canada**
Jaromir Jagr	**St. Alban's, Vermont, USA**
Ed Belfour	**Maniwaki, Quebec, Canada**
Theoren Fleury	**Hay River, Northwest Territories, Canada**
Tony Granato	**Downers Grove, Illinois, USA**
Jere Lehtinen	**Inverness, Nova Scotia, Canada**
Mark Recchi	**Kamloops, British Columbia, Canada**
John LeClair	**Kladno, Czech Republic**

YOU MAKE THE CALL

Most NHL players are now over six feet tall, weigh around 200 pounds, skate as fast as the wind and shoot the puck at speeds up to 100 miles per hour. In addition, they cross-check, fight, hold, trip, knee, spear, highstick and generally do whatever they can to make life miserable for the other team — and the referee.

No doubt about it, it's tough to be a referee. You must have the ability to make split-second decisions, even if 20,000 screaming fans think you've made the wrong call.

To test how well you'd do as a referee, answer yes or no to the following questions:

1. On a penalty shot, if the goalie makes the initial save but gives up a rebound, can the player shoot again and score?

   ❑ Yes ☑ No

2. If a player tries to trick the referee into calling a penalty by taking a dive, can they be penalized?

   ☑ Yes ❑ No

3. If a coach falls over the boards onto the ice during play, would his team be called for too many men on the ice?

   ❑ Yes ☑ No

4. If a goalie takes a major penalty — i.e. for slashing, high sticking or fighting — can that goalie stay in the game and have a teammate serve the penalty?

   ☑ Yes ❑ No

HOCKEY RULES

The game of ice hockey has seen many changes over the years and so have the rules — probably because some of them were so strange! Here's a collection of some of the oddest rules:

- Prior to the start of the 1917-18 season, if a goalie dropped to the ice to block a shot, he was given a warning. If it happened again, he was fined two dollars and put in the penalty box for five minutes.
- Goal judges used to stand on the ice right behind the net.
- Until 1921-22, all minor penalties were three minutes long.
- Until 1927-28, no forward passes were allowed in the defending and neutral zones — players had to carry the puck forward.

- Until 1931-32, it was legal to play two goalies in the net at the same time, although there is no record of any team actually doing this.
- Prior to the 1938-39 season, players taking a penalty shot weren't allowed to skate in on the goalie. Instead, they had to shoot from behind a line 38 feet from the goal.
- The 1992-93 season was the first in which a minor penalty for diving was introduced.

ANSWERS

Logo Lingo (page 7)

Washington: Eagle
Montreal: The letters C and H
Ottawa: Roman soldier
Nashville: Sabre-tooth tiger
St. Louis: Musical note
Calgary: Logo on fire
Edmonton: A drip
Los Angeles: Crown
Vancouver: Killer whale
San Jose: Broken hockey stick
New York Rangers: Statue of Liberty

New team's name: Atlanta Thrashers

Top Guns (pages 8-9)

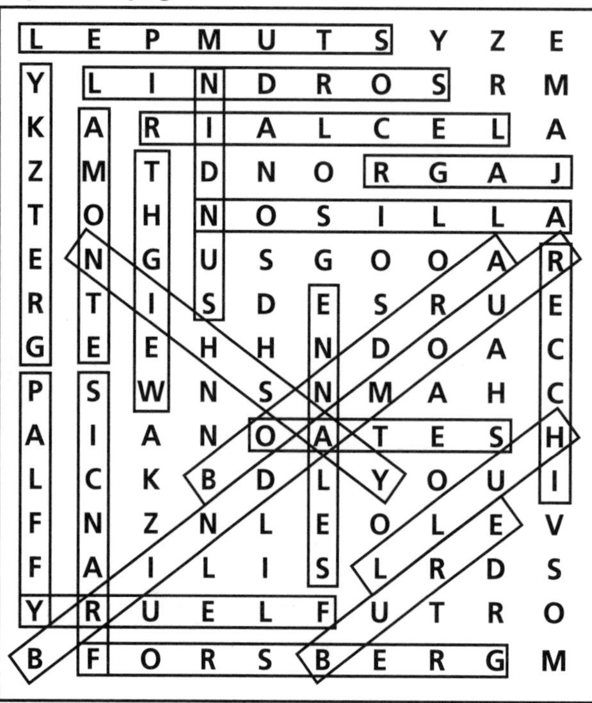

Five Stanley Cup-winning Detroit Red Wings:
- Yzerman
- Osgood
- Shanahan
- Kozlov
- Lidstrom

Common Ground (pages 11-12)

1) They all played hockey for Finland in the 1998 Winter Olympics.
2) All of them have been both NHL players and coaches.
3) They've all played goal in the NHL.
4) They've all played on the Los Angeles Kings team.
5) They all won medals in the 1998 Winter Olympics.
6) They've all won the Jack Adams trophy for coach of the year.
7) All of the above.
8) They've all played professional hockey in Europe.

Faces of Hockey (page 13)

1) Gino Odjick
2) Sergei Fedorov
3) Mats Sundin
4) Judy Diduck
5) Mike Modano
6) Cammi Granato

Who Am I (page 20)

Hayley Wickenheiser

Gone But Not Forgotten (page 21)

Philadelphia Quakers
Montreal Maroons
Cleveland Barons
California/Oakland Seals
Atlanta Flames
Colorado Rockies
Quebec Nordiques
Pittsburgh Pirates
Hartford Whalers
Kansas City Scouts
Minnesota North Stars

The flaming A was the logo of the Atlanta Flames.

Hockey Stars (pages 22-23)

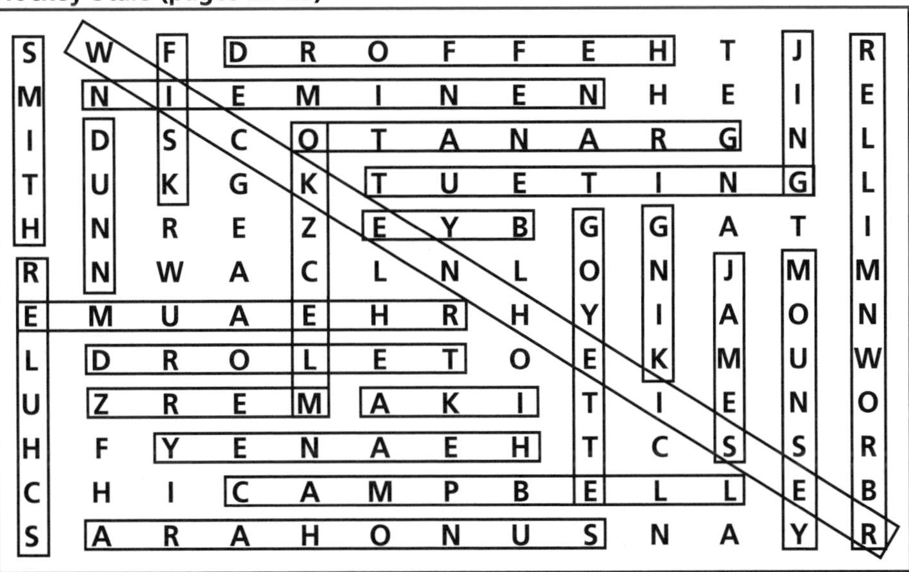

Nickname of Guo Hong: The Great Wall of China

Bringing Home the Hardware (pages 24-25)

1) Pavel Bure
2) $10,000
3) Abby Hoffman
4) Jack Adams
5) The goalkeeper(s) having played a minimum of 25 games for the team with the fewest goals scored against it.
6) Dionne scored more goals.
7) The team with the best regular-season record.

Puzzling Pictures (page 26)

1) Joe Thornton
2) Steve Yzerman
3) Russian Rocket
4) Doug Weight
5) Stu Barnes
6) Joe Sakic
7) Mark Messier

It's a Numbers Game (page 27)

Record for most goals in a career: 885
Longest undefeated streak by a team: 35
Most penalty minutes in a career: 3,966
Fewest home losses in a modern-day season (70+ games): 1
Number of players drafted in 1998 entry draft: 258
Most points in a period: 6
Most games played in a career: 1,767
Number of registered women hockey players in North America: 53,317
Most Hart Trophies won by one player: 10
Most shut-outs in a career: 103
Most 20+ goal-scorers on one team in a year: 11
Most games coached by one coach: 1,818
Fewest seconds it took for a rookie to score in his first game in the NHL: 15

Total Trivia (page 35)

1) Saskatoon
2) Jovocop
3) Dyed their hair blonde
4) George Hainsworth
5) As of the end of the 1997-98 season, no expansion team had ever had a winning record
6) Darryl Sittler
7) Lost weight
8) Olaf Kolzig
9) Dick Irvin

It's a Family Game (page 38)

1) Pavel and Valeri Bure
2) Russ and Geoff Courtnall
3) Rob and Scott Niedermayer
4) Boris and Dmitri Mironov
5) Wayne and Keith Primeau

From Small-Town Rinks (page 43)

Curtis Joseph: Kleswick, Ontario, Canada
Gino Odjick: Maniwaki, Quebec, Canada
Al MacInnis: Inverness, Nova Scotia, Canada
Peter Forsberg: Ornskoldsvik, Sweden
Geoff Sanderson: Hay River, NWT, Canada
Steve Yzerman: Cranbrook, BC, Canada
Jaromir Jagr: Kladno, Czech Republic
Ed Belfour: Carman, Manitoba, Canada
Theoren Fleury: Oxbow, Saskatchewan, Canada
Tony Granato: Downers Grove, Illinois, USA
Jere Lehtinen: Espoo, Finland
Mark Recchi: Kamloops, BC, Canada
John LeClair: St. Alban's, Vermont, USA

You Make the Call (page 44)

1) No
2) Yes
3) No
4) Yes